THE JOURNEY TO THE EAST

*

Books by Hermann Hesse

Peter Camenzind
Beneath the Wheel
Gertrude
Rosshalde
Knulp
Demian
Strange News from Another Star
Klingsor's Last Summer
Wandering
Siddhartha
Steppenwolf
Narcissus and Goldmund
The Journey to the East
The Glass Bead Game
If the War Goes On . . .
Poems
Autobiographical Writings
Stories of Five Decades
My Belief
Reflections
Crisis
Tales of Student Life
Hours in the Garden
Pictor's Metamorphoses
Soul of the Age: Selected Letters of Hermann Hesse

PICADOR

FARRAR, STRAUS AND GIROUX

NEW YORK

THE JOURNEY TO THE EAST

✳

HERMANN

HESSE

Translated by Hilda Rosner

www.picadorusa.com

Picador ® is a U.S. registered trademark and is used by
Farrar, Straus and Giroux under license from Pan Books Limited.

For information on Picador Reading Group Guides, as well as ordering,
please contact the Trade Marketing department at St. Martin's Press.
Phone: 1-800-221-7945 extension 763
Fax: 212-677-7456
E-mail: trademarketing@stmartins.com

ISBN 0-312-42168-0

First published in Germany under the title *Die Morgenlandfahrt*

15 16 17 18 19 20

THE
JOURNEY
TO THE
EAST

*

I

It was my destiny to join in a great experience. Having had the good fortune to belong to the League, I was permitted to be a participant in a unique journey. What wonder it had at the time! How radiant and comet-like it seemed, and how quickly it has been forgotten and allowed to fall into disrespute. For this reason, I have decided to attempt a short description of this fabulous journey, a journey the like of which had not been attempted since the days

of Hugo and mad Roland. Ours have been remarkable times, this period since the World
War, troubled and confused, yet, despite this,
fertile. I do not think that I am under any illusion about the difficulties of my attempt; they
are very great and are not only of a subjective
nature, although these alone would be consid-
erable. For not only do I no longer possess the
tokens, mementos, documents and diaries relating to the journey, but in the difficult years of
misfortune, sickness and deep affliction which
have elapsed since then, a large number of my
recollections have also vanished. As a result of
the buffets of Fate and because of the continual
discouragement, my memory as well as my
confidence in these earlier vivid recollections
have become impaired. But apart from these
purely personal notes, I am handicapped because of my former vow to the League; for
although this vow permits unrestricted com-
munication of my personal experiences, it for-
bids any disclosures about the League itself.
And even though the League seems to have
had no visible existence for a long time and I
have not seen any of its members again, no al-

lurement or threat in the world would induce me to break my vow. On the contrary, if today or tomorrow I had to appear before a court-martial and was given the option of dying or divulging the secret of the League, I would joyously seal my vow to the League with death.

It can be noted here that since the travel diary of Count Keyserling, several books have appeared in which the authors, partly unconsciously, but also partly deliberately, have given the impression that they are brothers of the League and had taken part in the Journey to the East. Incidentally, even the adventurous travel accounts of Ossendowski come under this justifiable suspicion. But they all have nothing to do with the League and our Journey to the East, or at any rate, no more than ministers of a small sanctimonious sect have to do with the Saviour, the Apostles and the Holy Ghost to whom they refer for special favor and membership. Even if Count Keryserling really sailed round the world with ease, and if Ossendowski actually traversed the countries he described, yet their journeys were not remarkable and they discovered no new territory, whereas at certain stages of our Journey to the East, although the commonplace aids of modern travel such as railways, steamers, telegraph, automobiles, airplanes, etc., were renounced, we penetrated into the heroic and magical. It was shortly after the World War, and the beliefs of the conquered nations were in an extraordinary state of unreality. There was a readiness to believe in things beyond reality even though only a few barriers were actually overcome and few advances made into the realm of a future psychiatry. Our journey at that time across the Moon Ocean to Famagusta under the leadership of Albert the Great, or say, the discovery of the Butterfly Island, twelve leagues beyond Zipangu, or the inspiring league ceremony at Rudiger's grave—those were deeds and experiences which were allotted once only to people of our time and zone.

I see that I am already coming up against one of the greatest obstacles in my account. The heights to which our deeds rose, the spiritual plane of experience to which they belong might be made proportionately more comprehensible to the reader if I were permitted to disclose to him the essence of the League's secret. But a great deal, perhaps everything, will remain incredible and incomprehensible. One paradox, however, must be accepted and this is that it is necessary to continually attempt the seemingly impossible. I agree with Siddhartha, our wise friend from the East, who once said: "Words do not express thoughts very well; everything immediately becomes a little different, a little distorted, a little foolish. And yet it also pleases me and seems right that what is of value and wisdom to one man seems nonsense to another." Even centuries ago the members and historians of our League recognized and courageously faced up to this difficulty. One of the greatest of them gave expression to it in an immortal verse:

"He who travels far will often see things
Far removed from what he believed was Truth.
When he talks about it in the fields at home,
He is often accused of lying,
For the obdurate people will not believe

What they do not see and distinctly feel.
Inexperience, I believe,
Will give little credence to my song."

This inexperience has also created the position where, now that publicity is being given to our journey which once roused thousands to ecstasy, it is not only forgotten but a real taboo is imposed upon its recollection. History is rich in examples of a similar kind. The whole of world history often seems to me nothing more than a picture book which portrays humanity's most powerful and senseless desire—the desire to forget. Does not each generation, by means of suppression, concealment and ridicule, efface what the previous generation considered most important? Have we not just had the experience that a long, horrible, monstrous war has been forgotten, gainsaid, distorted and dismissed by all nations? And now that they have had a short respite, are not the same nations trying to recall by means of exciting war novels what they themselves caused and endured a few years ago? In the same way, the day of rediscovery will come for the deeds and sor-

rows of our League, which are now either forgotten or are a laughingstock in the world,
and my notes should make a small contribu-
tion towards it.

One of the characteristics of the Journey to
the East was that although the League aimed
at quite definite, very lofty goals during this
journey (they belong to the secret category and
are therefore not communicable), yet every
single participant could have his own private
goals. Indeed, he had to have them; for no one
was included who did not have such private
goals, and every single one of us, while appear-
ing to share common ideals and goals and to
fight under a common flag, carried his own
fond childhood dream within his heart as a
source of inner strength and comfort. My own
goal for the journey, about which the President
questioned me before my acceptance into the
League, was a simple one, but many members
of the League had set themselves goals which,
although I respected, I could not fully understand. For example, one of them was a treas-
ure-seeker and he thought of nothing else but
of winning a great treasure which he called

"'Tao.'" Still another had conceived the idea of capturing a certain snake to which he attributed magical powers and which he called Kundalini. My own journey and life-goal, which had colored my dreams since my late boyhood, was to see the beautiful Princess Fatima and, if possible, to win her love.

At the time that I had the good fortune to join the League—that is, immediately after the end of the World War—our country was full of saviors, prophets and disciples, of presentiments about the end of the world, or hopes for the dawn of a Third Empire. Shattered by the war, in despair as a result of deprivation and hunger, greatly disillusioned by the seeming futility of all the sacrifices in blood and goods, our people at that time were lured by many phantoms, but there were also many real spiritual advances. There were Bacchanalian dance societies and Anabaptist groups, there was one thing after another that seemed to point to what was wonderful and beyond the veil. There was also at that time a widespread leaning towards Indian, ancient Persian and other Eastern mysteries and religions, and all this gave most people the impression that our ancient League was one of the many newly-blossomed cults, and that after a few years it would also be partly forgotten, despised and decried. The faithful amongst its disciples cannot dispute this.

How well do I remember the hour when, after the expiration of my probation year, I presented myself before the High Throne. I was given insight to the project of the Journey to the East, and after I had dedicated myself, body and soul, to this project, I was asked in a friendly way what I personally hoped to gain from this journey into the legendary realm. Although blushing somewhat, I confessed frankly and unhesitatingly to the assembled officials that it was my heart's desire to be allowed to see Princess Fatima. The Speaker, interpreting the allusion, gently placed his hand on my head and uttered the formula which confirmed my admission as a member of the League. "Anima pia," he said and bade me be constant in faith, courageous in danger, and to love my fellow-men. Well-schooled during my year's probation, I took the oath, renounced the world and its superstitions and had the League ring placed on my finger to the words from one of the most beautiful chapters in our League's history:

"On earth and in the air, in water and in fire,
The spirits are subservient to him,
His glance frightens and tames the wildest
   beasts,
And even the anti-Christian must approach
   him with awe. . . . etc."

To my great pleasure, immediately on admission to the League, we novitiates were given insight to our prospects. For instance, on following the directions of the officials to attach myself to one of the groups of ten people who were en route throughout the country to join the League's expedition, one of the League's secrets immediately became vividly clear to me. I realized that I had joined a pilgrimage to the East, seemingly a definite and single pilgrimage—but in reality, in its broadest sense, this expedition to the East was not only mine and now; this procession of believers and disciples had always and incessantly been moving towards the East, towards the Home of Light. Throughout the centuries it had been on the way, towards light and wonder, and each member, each group, indeed our whole host and its great pilgrimage, was only a wave in the eternal stream of human beings, of the eternal strivings of the human spirit towards the East, towards Home. The knowledge passed through my mind like a ray of light and immediately reminded me of a phrase which I had learned during my novitiate year, which had always pleased me immensely without my realizing its full significance. It was a phrase by the poet Novalis, "Where are we really going? Always home!"

Meantime, our group had set off on its travels; soon we encountered other groups, and the feeling of unity and a common goal gave us increasing happiness. Faithful to our instructions, we lived like pilgrims and made no use of those contrivances which spring into existence in a world deluded by money, number and time, and which drain life of its content; mechanical contrivances such as railways.

watches and the like came chiefly into this category. Another unanimously observed rule bade us visit and pay homage to all places and associations relating to the ancient history of our League and its faith. We visited and honored all sacred places and monuments, churches and consecrated tombstones which we came across on our way; chapels and altars were adorned with flowers; ruins were honored with songs or silent contemplation; the dead were commemorated with music and prayers. It was not unusual for us to be mocked at and disturbed by unbelievers, but it also happened often enough that priests blessed us and invited us to be their guests, that children enthusiastically joined us, learned our songs and saw us depart with tears in their eyes; that an old man would show us forgotten monuments or tell us a legend about his district; that youths would walk with us part of the way and desire to join the League. The latter were given advice and apprised of the first rites and practices of novitiates. We were aware of the first wonders, partly through seeing them with our own eyes and partly through unexpected accounts and legends. One day, when I was still quite a new member, someone suddenly mentioned that the giant Agramant was a guest in our leaders' tent, and was trying to persuade them to make their way across Africa in order to liberate some League members from Moorish captivity. Another time we saw the Goblin, the pitch-maker, the comforter, and we presumed that we should make our way towards the Blue Pot. However, the first amazing phenomenon which I saw with my own eyes was when we had stopped for prayer and rest at an old half-ruined Chapel in the region of Spaichendorf; on the only undamaged wall of the Chapel there was painted a very large picture of Saint Christopher, and on his shoulder, small, and half-faded from old age, sat the Child Saviour. The leaders, as was sometimes their custom, did not simply propose the direction we should take, but invited us all to give our opinion, for the Chapel lay at a three-direction signpost and we had the choice. Only a few of us expressed a wish or gave advice, but one person pointed to the left and urgently requested that we should choose this path. We were all silent then and waited for our leaders' decision, when Saint Christopher raised his arm holding the long, thick staff and pointed to the left where our brother desired to go. We all watched this in silence, and silently the leaders turned to the left and went along this path, and we all followed with the utmost pleasure.

We had not been long on our way in Swabia when a power which we had not thought about became noticeable. We had felt its influence strongly for rather a long time without quite knowing whether it was friendly or hostile. It was the power of the guardians of the crown who, since olden times, had preserved the memory and inheritance of the Hohenstaufen in that country. I do not know whether our leaders knew more about it and had any instructions regarding it. I only know that we received many exhortations and warnings from them, such as on the hill on the way to Bopfingen where we met a hoary old warrior; he shook his grey head with his eyes closed and disappeared again without leaving any trace. Our leaders took notice of the warning;

we turned back and did not go to Bopfingen. On the other hand, it happened in the neighborhood of Urach that an ambassador of the crown guardians appeared in our leaders' tent as if sprung from out of the ground, and with promises and threats tried to induce them to put our expedition at the service of the Staufen, and indeed to make preparations for the conquest of Sicily. When the leaders firmly refused this demand, he said he would put a dreadful curse on the League and on our expedition. And yet I am only reporting what was whispered among ourselves; the leaders themselves did not mention a word about it. Still, it seems possible that it was our uncertain relationship with the guardians of the crown which, for a long time, gave our League the unmerited reputation of being a secret society for the restoration of the monarchy.

On one occasion I also had the experience of seeing one of my comrades entertain doubts; he renounced his vow and relapsed into disbelief. He was a young man whom I had liked very much. His personal reason for joining the expedition to the East was his desire to see the coffin of the prophet Mohammed from which, it had been said, he could by magic rise freely into the air. In one of those Swabian or Ale-mannic small towns where we stopped for a few days, because an opposition of Saturn and the moon checked our progress, this unfortu-nate man, who had seemed sad and restless for some time, met one of his former teachers to whom he had remained very attached since his schooldays. This teacher was successful in again making the young man see our cause in the light which it appears to unbelievers. After one of these visits to the teacher, the poor man came back to our camp in a dreadful state of excitement and with a distorted countenance. He made a commotion outside the leaders' tent, and when the Speaker came out he shouted at him angrily that he had had enough of this ridiculous expedition which would never bring us to the East; he had had enough of the journey being interrupted for days be-cause of stupid astrological considerations; he was more than tired of idleness, of childish wanderings, of floral ceremonies, of attaching importance to magic, of the intermingling of life and poetry; he would throw the ring at the leaders' feet, take his leave and return by the trusty railway to his home and his useful work. It was an ugly and lamentable sight. We were filled with shame and yet at the same time pitied the misguided man. The Speaker listened to him kindly, stooped with a smile for the discarded ring, and said in a quiet, cheerful voice which must have put the blustering man to shame: "You have said good-bye to us and want to return to the railway, to common-sense and useful work. You have said good-bye to the League, to the expedition to the East, good-bye to magic, to floral festivals, to poetry. You are absolved from your vow."

"Also from the vow of silence?" cried the deserter.

"Yes, also from the vow of silence," answered the Speaker. "Remember, you vowed to keep silent about the secret of the League to unbelievers. As we see you have forgotten the secret, you will not be able to pass it on to anyone."

"I have forgotten something! I have forgotten nothing," cried the young man, but became uncertain, and as the Speaker turned his back on him and withdrew to the tent, he suddenly ran quickly away.

We were sorry, but the days were crammed so full with events that I quickly forgot him. But it happened some time later, when none of us thought about him any more, that we heard the inhabitants of several villages and towns through which we passed, talk about this same youth. A young man had been there (and they described him accurately and mentioned his name) who had been looking for us everywhere. First he had said that he belonged to us, had stayed behind on the journey and had lost his way. Then he began to weep and stated that he had been unfaithful to us and had run away, but now he realized that he could no longer live outside the League; he wished to, and indeed must, find us in order to go down on his knees before the leaders and beg to be forgiven. We heard this tale told again here, there, and everywhere; wherever we went, the wretched man had just been there. We asked the Speaker what he thought about it and what would be the outcome. "I do not think that he will find us," said the Speaker briefly. And he did not find us. We did not see him again.

Once, when one of the leaders had drawn me into a confidential conversation, I gathered courage and asked him how things stood with this renegade brother. After all, he was penitent and was looking for us, I said; we ought to help him redeem his error. No doubt, he would in the future be the most loyal member of the League. The leader said: "We should be happy if he did find his way back to us, but we cannot aid him. He has made it very difficult for himself to have faith again. I fear that he would not see and recognize us even if we passed close by him; he has become blind. Repentance alone does not help. Grace cannot be bought with repentance; it cannot be bought at all. A similar thing has already happened to many other people; great and famous men have shared the same fate as this young man. Once in their youth the light shone for them; they saw the light and followed the star, but then came reason and the mockery of the world; then came faint-heartedness and apparent failure; then came weariness and disillusionment, and so they lost their way again, they became blind again. Some of them have spent the rest of their lives looking for us again, but could not find us. They have then told the world that our League is only a pretty legend and people should not be misled by it. Others have become our deadly enemies and have abused and harmed the League in every possible way."

There were wonderful festive days each time we encountered other parties of the League's hosts on our way; sometimes we then formed a camp of hundreds, even thousands. The expedition did not, in fact, proceed in any fixed order with participants moving in the same direction in more or less closed columns. On the contrary, numerous groups were simultaneously on the way, each following their own leaders and their own stars, each one always ready to merge into a greater unit and belong to it for a time, but always no less ready to move on again separately. Some went on their way quite alone. I also walked alone at times,

whenever some sign or call tempted me to go
my own way.

I remember a select little group with which
we traveled and camped together for some
days; this group had undertaken to liberate
some captive League brothers and the Princess
Isabella from the hands of the Moors. It was
said that they were in possession of Hugo's
horn, and among them were my friends the
poet Lauscher and the artists Klingsor and
Paul Klee; they spoke of nothing else but
Africa and the captured princess, and their
Bible was the book of the deeds of Don Quixote, in whose honor they thought of making
their way across Spain.

It was very pleasant whenever we met one
of these groups, to attend their feasts and devotions and to invite them to ours, to hear about
their deeds and plans, to bless and know them
on parting; they went their way, we went ours.
Each one of them had his own dream, his wish,
his secret heart's desire, and yet they all flowed
together in the great stream and all belonged
to each other, shared the same reverence and

the same faith, and had made the same vow! I met Jup, the magician, who proposed to gather the fortune of his life in Kashmir; I met Collo-fine, the sorcerer, quoting his favorite passage from the Adventures of Simplicissimus; I met Louis the Terrible, who dreamt of planting an olive-grove in the Holy Land and keeping slaves. He went arm-in-arm with Anselm, who was in search of the purple iris of his childhood. I met and loved Ninon, known as "the foreigner." Dark eyes gleamed beneath her black hair. She was jealous of Fatima, the princess of my dreams, and yet she was prob-ably Fatima herself without my knowing it. And as we moved on, so had once pilgrims, emperors and crusaders moved on to liberate the Saviour's grave, or to study Arabian magic; Spanish knights had traveled this way, as well as German scholars, Irish monks and French poets.

I, whose calling was really only that of a violinist and story-teller, was responsible for the provision of music for our group, and I then discovered how a long time devoted to small details exalts us and increases our strength. I did not only play the violin and conduct our choirs, but also collected old songs and chorals. I wrote motets and madrigals for six and eight voices and practised them. But I will not give you details of these.

I was very fond of many of my comrades and leaders, but not one of them subsequently occupied my thoughts as much as Leo, while at that time he was apparently hardly noticed. Leo was one of our servants (who were naturally volunteers, as we were). He helped to carry the luggage and was often assigned to the personal service of the Speaker. This unaffected man had something so pleasing, so unobtrusively winning about him that everyone loved him. He did his work gaily, usually sang or whistled as he went along, was never seen except when needed—in fact, an ideal servant. Furthermore, all animals were attached to him. We nearly always had some dog or other with us which joined us on account of Leo; he could tame birds and attract butterflies to him. It was his desire for Solomon's key which would enable him to understand the language of the birds that had drawn him to the East.

This servant Leo worked in a very simple and natural manner, friendly in an unassuming way, alongside the many forms of our League, which, without doing harm to the value and sincerity of the League, had within them something exalting, something singular, solemn, or fantastic. What makes my account particularly difficult is the great disparity in my individual recollections. I have already said that sometimes we marched along only as a small group; sometimes we formed a troop or even an army, but sometimes I remained in a district with only a few friends, or even quite alone, without tents, without leaders and without a Speaker. My tale becomes even more difficult because we not only wandered through Space, but also through Time. We moved towards the East, but we also traveled into the Middle Ages and the Golden Age; we roamed through Italy or Switzerland, but at times we also spent the night in the 10th century and dwelt with the patriarchs or the fairies. During the times I remained alone, I often found again places and people of my own past. I wandered with my former betrothed along the edges of the forest of the Upper Rhine, caroused with friends of my youth in Tübingen, in Basle or in Florence, or I was a boy and went with my school-friends to catch butterflies or to watch an otter, or my company consisted of the beloved characters of my books; Almansor and Parsifal, Witiko or Goldmund rode by my side, or Sancho Panza, or we were guests at the Barmekides. When I found my way back to our group in some valley or another, heard the League's songs and camped by the leaders' tents, it was immediately clear to me that my excursion into my childhood and my ride with Sancho belonged essentially to this journey. For our goal was not only the East, or rather the East was not only a country and something geographical, but it was the home and youth of the soul, it was everywhere and nowhere, it was the union of all times. Yet I was only aware of this for a moment, and therein lay the reason for my great happiness at that time. Later, when I had lost this happiness again, I clearly understood these connections without deriving the slightest benefit or comfort from them. When something precious and irretrievable is lost, we have the feeling of having awakened from a dream. In my case this feeling is strangely correct, for my happiness did indeed arise from the same secret as the happiness in dreams; it arose from the freedom to experience everything imaginable simultaneously, to exchange outward and inward easily, to move Time and Space about like scenes in a theatre. And as we League brothers traveled throughout the world without motor-cars or ships, as we conquered the war-shattered world by our faith and transformed it into Paradise, we creatively brought the past, the future and the fictitious into the present moment.

And again and again, in Swabia, at Bodensee, in Switzerland, everywhere, we met people who understood us, or were in some way thankful that we and our League and our Journey to the East existed. Amid the tramways and banks of Zürich we came across Noah's Ark guarded by several old dogs which all had the same name, and which were bravely guided across the shallow waters of a calm period by Hans C. to Noah's descendant, to the friend of the arts. We went to Winterthur, down into Stocklin's Magic Closet; we were guests in the Chinese Temple where the incense holders gleamed beneath the bronze Maja and the black king played the flute sweetly to the vibrating tone of the temple gong. And at the foot of the Sun Mountains we came across Suon Mali, a colony of the King of Siam, where, amongst the stone and brazen Buddhas, we offered up our libations and incense as grateful guests.

One of the most beautiful experiences was the League's celebration in Bremgarten; the magic circle surrounded us closely there. Received by Max and Tilli, the lords of the castle, we heard Othmar play Mozart on the grandpiano in the lofty hall. We found the grounds occupied by parrots and other talking birds. We heard the fairy Armida sing at the fountain. With blown locks the heavy head of the astrologer Longus nodded by the side of the beloved countenance of Henry of Ofterdingen. In the garden, the peacocks screeched, and Louis conversed in Spanish with Puss in Boots, while Hans Resom, shaken after his peeps into the masked game of life, vowed he would go on a pilgrimage to the grave of Charles the Great. It was one of the triumphant periods of our journey; we had brought the magic wave with us; it cleansed everything. The native paid homage on his knees to beauty, the lord of the castle produced a poem which dealt with our evening activities. The animals from the forest lurked close to the castle walls, and in the river the gleaming fishes moved in lively swarms and were fed with cakes and wine.

The best of these experiences really worth relating are those which reflect the spirit of it. My description of them seems poor and perhaps foolish, but everyone who participated in and celebrated the days at Bremgarten would confirm every single detail and supplement them with hundreds which are more beautiful. I shall always remember how the peacocks' tails shimmered when the moon rose amongst the tall trees, and on the shady bank the emerging mermaids gleamed fresh and silvery amongst the rocks; how Don Quixote stood alone under the chestnut-tree by the fountain

and held his first night-watch while the last
Roman candles of the firework display fell so
softly over the castle's turrets in the moonlight,
and my colleague Pablo, adorned with roses,
played the Persian reed-pipe to the girls. Oh,
which of us ever thought that the magic circle
would break up so soon! That almost all of us
—and also I, even I—should again lose myself
in the soundless deserts of mapped out reality,
just like officials and shop-assistants who, after
a party or a Sunday outing, adapt themselves
again to everyday business life!

In those days none of us was capable of such
thoughts. From the castle's turrets of Bremgarten, the fragrance of lilac entered my bed-
room. I heard the river flowing beyond the
trees. I climbed out of the window in the
depth of the night, intoxicated with happiness
and yearning. I stole past the knight on guard
and the sleeping banqueters down to the river-
bank, to the flowing waters, to the white,
gleaming mermaids. They took me down with
them into the cool, moonlit crystal world of
their home, where they played dreamily with
the crowns and golden chains from their treas-

ure-chambers. It seemed to me that I spent months in the sparkling depths and when I emerged and swam ashore, thoroughly chilled, Pablo's reed-pipe was still to be heard from the garden far away, and the moon was still high in the sky. I saw Leo playing with two white poodles, his clever, boyish face radiating happiness. I found Longus sitting in the wood. On his knees was a book of parchment in which he was writing Greek and Hebrew characters; dragons flew out of the letters, and colored snakes reared themselves. He did not look at me; he went on painting, absorbed in his colored snake-writing. For a long time I looked over his bent shoulders into the book. I saw the snakes and dragons emerge from his writing, whirl about and silently disappear into the dark wood. "Longus," I said to him softly, "dear friend!" He did not hear me, my world was far from his. And quite apart, under the moonlit trees, Anselm wandered about with an iris in his hand; lost in thought, he stared and smiled at the flower's purple calyx.

Something that I had observed several times during our journey, without having fully con-

sidered it, impressed me again during the days
at Bremgarten, strangely and rather painfully.
There were amongst us many artists, painters,
musicians and poets. Ardent Klingsor was
there and restless Hugo Wolf, taciturn
Lauscher and vivacious Brentano—but however animated and lovable the personalites of
these artists were, yet without exception their
imaginary characters were more animated,
more beautiful, happier and certainly finer and
more real than the poets and creators themselves. Pablo sat there with his flute in enchant-
ing innocence and joy, but his poet slipped
away like a shadow to the river-bank, half-
transparent in the moonlight, seeking solitude.
Stumbling and rather drunk, Hoffman ran
here and there amongst the guests, talking a
great deal, small and elfish, and he also, like
all of them, was only half-real, only half there,
not quite solid, not quite real. At the same
time, the archivist Lindhorst, playing at
dragons for a joke, continually breathed fire
and discharged energy like an automobile. I
asked the servant Leo why it was that artists
sometimes appeared to be only half-alive,

while their creations seemed so irrefutably alive. Leo looked at me, surprised at my question. Then he released the poodle he was holding in his arms and said: "It is just the same with mothers. When they have borne their children and given them their milk and beauty and strength, they themselves become invisible, and no one asks about them any more."

"But that is sad," I said, without really thinking very much about it.

"I do not think it is sadder than all other things," said Leo. "Perhaps it is sad and yet also beautiful. The law ordains that it shall be so."

"The law?" I asked curiously. "What law is that, Leo?"

"The law of service. He who wishes to live long must serve, but he who wishes to rule does not live long."

"Then why do so many strive to rule?"

"Because they do not understand. There are few who are born to be masters; they remain happy and healthy. But all the others who have only become masters through endeavor, end in nothing."

"In what nothing, Leo?"

"For example, in the sanitoria."

I understood little about it and yet the words remained in my memory and left me with a feeling that this Leo knew all kinds of things, that he perhaps knew more than us, who were ostensibly his masters.

II

Each participant in this unforgettable journey
had his own ideas as to what made our faithful
Leo suddenly decide to leave us in the middle
of the dangerous gorge of Morbio Inferiore. It
was only very much later that I began in some
measure to suspect and review the circumstances and deeper significance of this occur-
rence. It also seemed that this apparently
incidental but in reality extremely important
event, the disappearance of Leo, was in no way

an accident, but a link in that chain of events through which the eternal enemy sought to bring disaster to our undertaking. On that cool autumn morning when it was discovered that our servant Leo was missing and that all search for him remained fruitless, I was certainly not the only one who, for the first time, had a feeling of impending disaster and menacing destiny.

However, for the moment, this was the position. After we had boldly crossed half Europe and a portion of the Middle Ages, we camped in a very narrow rocky valley, a wild mountain gorge on the Italian border, and looked for the inexplicably missing Leo. The longer we looked for him and the more our hopes of finding him again dwindled during the course of the day, the more were we oppressed by the thought that it was not only the question of a popular, pleasant man amongst our servants who had either met with an accident or run away or had been captured by an enemy, but that this was the beginning of trouble, the first indication of a storm which would break over us. We spent the whole of the day, far into the twilight, searching for Leo. The whole of the gorge was explored, and while these exertions made us weary, and a feeling of hopelessness and futility grew amongst us all, it was very strange and uncanny how from hour to hour the missing servant seemed to increase in importance and our loss created difficulties. It was not only that each pilgrim, and without doubt the whole of the staff, were worried about the handsome, pleasant and willing youth, but it seemed that the more certain his loss became, the more indispensable he seemed; without Leo, his handsome face, his good humor and his songs, without his enthusiasm for our great undertaking, the undertaking itself seemed in some mysterious way to lose meaning. At least, that is how it affected me. Despite all the strain and many minor disillusionments during the previous months of the journey, I had never had a moment of inner weakness, of serious doubt; no successful general, no bird in the swallows' flight to Egypt, could be more sure of his goal, of his mission, of the rightness of his actions and aspirations than I was on this journey. But now, in this fateful place, while I

continually heard the calls and signals of our
sentinels during the whole of the blue and
golden October day, and awaited again and
again with growing excitement the arrival of
a report, only to suffer disappointment and to
gaze at perplexed faces, I had feelings of sadness and doubt for the first time. The stronger
these feelings became, the clearer it seemed to
me that it was not only that I had lost faith in
finding Leo again, but everything now seemed
to become unreliable and doubtful; the value
and meaning of everything was threatened:
our comradeship, our faith, our vow, our Journey to the East, our whole life.

Even if I was mistaken in presuming that
we all had these feelings, indeed even if I was
subsequently mistaken about my own feelings
and inner experiences and many things which
were in reality experienced much later and
erroneously attributed to that day, there still
remains, despite everything, the strange fact
about Leo's luggage. Quite apart from all personal moods, this was, in fact, rather strange,
fantastic, and an increasing source of worry.
Even during this day in the Morbio gorge,

even during our eager search for the missing
man, first one man, then another missed something important, something indispensable
from the luggage which could not be found
anywhere. It appeared that every missing article must have been in Leo's luggage, and although Leo, like all the rest of us, had only
carried the usual linen haversack on his back,
just one bag amongst about thirty others, it
seemed that in this one lost bag there were all
the really important things which we carried
with us on our journey. And although it is a
well-known human weakness that a thing at
the time we miss it has an exaggerated value
and seems less dispensable than the things we
have, and although the loss of many of the ar-
ticles which troubled us so much in the Morbio
gorge did, in fact, turn up again later, or finally
did not prove so indispensable—yet, despite all
this, it is unfortunately true that we did at that
time, with quite justifiable alarm, confirm the
loss of a whole series of extremely important
things.

The further extraordinary and singular
thing was this: the objects that were missing,

whether they appeared again later or not, assumed their importance by degrees, and gradually all the things believed lost, which we had wrongly missed so much and to which we had mistakenly attached so much importance, turned up again in our stores. In order to express here quite clearly what was true yet altogether inexplicable, it must be said that during the course of our further journey, tools, valuables, cards and documents which were all lost seemed, to our shame, to be indispensable. Quite frankly, it seemed as if each one of us stretched his entire imagination to persuade himself of terrible, irreplaceable losses, as if each one endeavored to conceive as lost that which was most important to him and to mourn over it; with one it was the passports, with another the maps, with another it was the Letter of Credit to the Caliph; it was this thing with one, that thing with another. And although in the end it was clear that one article after the other which was believed lost was either not lost at all or was unimportant or dispensable, there did remain one single thing that was really valuable, an inestimably important, absolutely fundamental and indispensable document that was really indisputably lost. But now opinions were ineffectually exchanged as to whether this document, which had disappeared with the servant Leo, had really been in our luggage. There was complete agreement about the great value of this document and that its loss was irreplaceable, and yet how few of us (amongst them myself) could declare with certainty that this document had been taken with us on the journey. One man asserted that a similar document had certainly been carried in Leo's linen bag; this was not the original document at all, but naturally only a copy; others declared that it had never been intended to take either the document itself or a copy on the journey, as this would have made a mockery of the whole meaning of our journey. This led to heated arguments and further demonstrated that there were various completely conflicting opinions about the whereabouts of the original (it was immaterial whether we only had the copy and whether we had lost it or not). The document, it was declared, was deposited with the government in

Kyffhäuser. No, said another, it lies buried in the urn which contains the ashes of our deceased master. Nonsense, said still another, the League document was drawn up by the master in the original characters known only to himself and it was burned with the master's corpse at his behest. Inquiries regarding the original document were meaningless, because after the master's death it was not possible for anyone to read it. But it was certainly necessary to ascertain where the four (some said six) translations of the original document were, which were made during the master's lifetime under his supervision. It was said that Chinese, Greek, Hebrew and Latin translations existed, and they were deposited in the four old capitals. Many other opinions and views were expressed; many clung obstinately to them, others were convinced first by one then by another opposing argument, and then soon changed their minds again. In brief, from that time, certainty and unity no longer existed in our community, although the great idea still kept us together.

How well I remember those first disputes! They were something so new and unheard-of in our hitherto perfectly united League. They were conducted with respect and politeness— at least at the beginning. At first they led neither to fierce conflicts nor personal reproaches or insults—at first we were still an inseparable, united brotherhood throughout the world. I still hear their voices, I still see our camping ground where the first of these debates was conducted. I see the golden autumn leaves falling here and there amongst the unusually serious faces. I see one on a knee, another lying on a hat. I listened, feeling more and more distressed and fearful, but amidst all the exchange of opinions I was inwardly quite sure of my belief, sadly sure; namely, that the original, genuine document had been in Leo's bag, and that it had disappeared and was lost with him. However gloomy this belief might be, still it was a belief. It was a firm one and gave me a feeling of certainty. At that time I truly thought that I would willingly exchange this belief for a more hopeful one. Only later, when I had lost this sad belief and was susceptible to all and sundry opinions, did I realize what I had possessed in my belief.

I see that the tale cannot be told in this way. But how can it be told, this tale of a unique journey, of a unique communion of minds, of such a wonderfully exalted and spiritual life? I should like so very much, as one of the last survivors of our community, to save some records of our great cause. I feel like the old surviving servant of perhaps one of the Paladins of Charles the Great, who recalls a stirring series of deeds and wonders, the images and memories of which will disappear with him if he is not successful in passing some of them on to posterity by means of word or picture, tale or song. But through what expedient is it possible to tell the story of the Journey to the East? I do not know. Already this first endeavor, this attempt begun with the best intentions, leads me into the boundless and incomprehensible. I simply wanted to try to depict what has remained in my memory of the course of events and individual details of our Journey to the East. Nothing seemed more simple. And now, when I have hardly related anything, I am brought to a halt by a single small episode which I had not originally thought of at all, the episode of Leo's disappearance. Instead of a fabric, I hold in my hands a bundle of a thousand knotted threads which would occupy hundreds of hands for years to disentangle and straighten out, even if every thread did not become terribly brittle and break between the fingers as soon as it is handled and gently drawn.

I imagine that every historian is similarly affected when he begins to record the events of some period and wishes to portray them sincerely. Where is the center of events, the common standpoint around which they revolve and which gives them cohesion? In order that something like cohesion, something like causality, that some kind of meaning might ensue and that it can in some way be narrated, the historian must invent units, a hero, a nation, an idea, and he must allow to happen to this invented unit what has in reality happened to the nameless.

If it is so difficult to relate connectedly a number of events which have really taken place and have been attested, it is in my case much more difficult, for everything becomes questionable as soon as I consider it closely, everything slips away and dissolves, just as our community, the strongest in the world, has been able to dissolve. There is no unit, no center, no point around which the wheel revolves.

Our Journey to the East and our League, the basis of our community, has been the most important thing, indeed the only important thing in my life, compared with which my own individual life has appeared completely unimportant. And now that I want to hold fast to and describe this most important thing, or at least something of it, everything is only a mass of separate fragmentary pictures which has been reflected in something, and this something is myself, and this self, this mirror, whenever I have gazed into it, has proved to be nothing but the uppermost surface of a glass plane. I put my pen away with the sincere intention and hope of continuing tomorrow or some other time, or rather to begin anew, but at the back of my intention and hope, at the back of my really tremendous urge to relate our story, there remains a dreadful doubt. It is the doubt that arose during the search for Leo in the valley of Morbio. This doubt does not only ask the question, "Is your story capable of being told?" It also asks the question, "Was it possible to experience it?" We recall examples of participants in the World War who, although by no means short of facts and attested stories, must at times have entertained the same doubts.

III

*

Since I wrote the foregoing, I have pondered over my project again and again and tried to find a way out of my difficulty. I have not found a solution. I am still confronted by chaos. But I have vowed not to give in, and in the moment of making this vow a happy memory passed through my mind like a ray of sunshine. It was similar, it seemed to me, quite similar to how I felt when we commenced our expedition; then also we undertook something apparently impossible, then also we apparently traveled in the dark, not knowing our direction and not having the slightest prospects. Yet we had within us something stronger than reality or probability, and that was faith in the meaning and necessity of our action. I shuddered at the recollection of this sentiment, and at the moment of this blissful shudder, everything became clear, everything seemed possible again.

Whatever happens, I have decided to exercise my will. Even if I have to re-commence my difficult story ten times, a hundred times, and always arrive at the same cul-de-sac, just the same I will begin again a hundred times. If I cannot assemble the pictures into a significant whole again, I will present each single fragment as faithfully as possible. And as far as it is now still possible, I will be mindful of the first principle of our great period, never to rely on and let myself be disconcerted by reason, always to know that faith is stronger than so-called reality.

In the meantime, I did make a sincere attempt to approach my goal in a practical and sensible manner. I went to see a friend of my youth who lives in this town and is editor of a newspaper. His name is Lukas. He had taken part in the World War and had published a book about it which had a large circulation. Lukas received me in a friendly manner. He was obviously pleased to see a former school-friend again. I had two long conversations with him.

I tried to make him understand my position. I scorned all evasion. I told him frankly that I was a participant in that great enterprise of which he must also have heard, in the so-called "Journey to the East," or the League expedition, or whatever it was then described as by the public. Oh yes, he smiled ironically, he certainly remembered it. In his circle of friends, this singular episode was mostly called, perhaps somewhat disrespectfully, "the Children's Crusade." This movement was not taken quite seriously in his circle. It had indeed been compared with some kind of theosophical movement or brotherhood. Just the same, they had been very surprised at the periodic successes of the undertaking. They had read with due respect about the courageous journey through Upper Swabia, of the triumph at Bremgarten, of the surrender of the Tessin mountain village, and had at times wondered whether the movement would like to place itself at the service of a republican government. Then, to be sure, the matter apparently petered out. Several of the former leaders left the movement; indeed, in some way they seemed to be ashamed of it and no longer wished to remember it. News about it came through very sparingly and it was always strangely contradictory, and so the whole matter was just placed aside *ad acta* and forgotten like so many eccentric political, religious or artistic movements of those post-war years. At that time so many prophets sprang up, so many secret societies with Messianic hopes appeared and then disappeared again leaving no trace.

His point of view was clear, it was that of a well-meaning sceptic. All others who had heard its story, but had not themselves taken part in it, probably thought the same about the League and the Journey to the East. It was not for me to convert Lukas, but I gave him some corrected information; for instance, that our League was in no way an off-shoot of the post-war years, but that it had extended throughout the whole of world history, sometimes, to be sure, under the surface, but in an unbroken line, that even certain phases of the World War were nothing else but stages in the history of our League; further, that Zoroaster, Lao Tse, Plato, Xenophon, Pythagoras, Albertus Magnus, Don Quixote, Tristram Shandy, Novalis and Baudelaire were cofounders and brothers of our League. He smiled exactly in the way that I expected.

"Well," I said, "I have not come here to instruct you, but to learn from you. It is my passionate desire to write, perhaps not a history of the League (even a whole army of well-equipped scholars would not be in a position to do this), but to tell quite simply the story of our journey. But I am quite unsuccessful in even approaching the subject. It is not a question of literary ability; I think I have this. Moreover, I have no ambitions in this respect. No, it is because the reality that I once experienced, together with my comrades, exists no longer, and although its memories are the most precious and vivid ones that I possess, they seem so far away, they are composed of such a different kind of fabric, that it seems as if they originated on other stars in other millennia, or as if they were hallucinations."

"I can understand that!" cried Lukas eagerly. Our conversation was only just beginning to interest him. "How well I understand! That is just how I was affected by my war experiences. I thought I had experienced them clearly and vividly, I was almost bursting with images of them; the roll of film in my head seemed miles long. But when I sat at my writing-desk, on a chair, by a table, the razed villages and woods, the earth tremors caused by heavy bombardment, the conglomeration of filth and greatness, of fear and heroism, of mangled stomachs and heads, of fear of death and grim humor, were all immeasurably remote, only a dream, were not related to anything and could not really be conceived. You know that despite this, I finally wrote my war-book and that it is now read and discussed a great deal. But do you know, I do not think

that ten books like it, each one ten times better and more vivid than mine, could convey
any real picture of the war to the most serious
reader, if he had not himself experienced the
war. And there were not so many who had.
Even those who participated in it did not for a
long time experience it. And if many really
did so—they forgot about it again. Next to the
hunger to experience a thing, men have perhaps no stronger hunger than to forget."

He was silent and looked perplexed and lost
in thought. His words had confirmed my
own experiences and thoughts.

After a time I asked him warily, "Then how
was it possible for you to write the book?"

He thought for a moment, brought back
from his reflections. "It was only possible for
me to do it," he said, "because it was necessary.
I either had to write the book or be reduced to
despair; it was the only means of saving me
from nothingness, chaos and suicide. The book
was written under this pressure and brought
me the expected cure, simply because it was
written, irrespective of whether it was good or
bad. That was the only thing that counted.

And while writing it, there was no need for me to think at all of any other reader but myself, or at the most, here and there another close war-comrade, and I certainly never thought then about the survivors, but always about those who fell in the war. While writing it, I was as if delirious or crazy, surrounded by three or four people with mutilated bodies— that is how the book was produced."

And suddenly he said—it was the end of our first conversation: "Forgive me, I cannot say any more about it, not a single word more. I cannot, I will not. Good-bye."

He pushed me out.

At our second meeting he was again calm and collected, had the same ironical smile and yet seemed to treat my problem seriously and to understand it fully. He made a few suggestions which seemed, however, of little use to me. At the end of the second and last conversation, he said to me almost casually:

"Listen, you continually come back to the episode with the servant Leo. I do not like it; it seems to be an obstacle in your way. Free yourself, throw Leo overboard; he seems to be becoming a fixed idea."

I wanted to reply that one could not write any books without fixed ideas. Instead he startled me with the quite unexpected question: "Was he really called Leo?"

There was perspiration on my brow.

"Yes," I said, "of course he was called Leo."

"Was that his Christian name?"

I stammered.

"No, his Christian name was—was—I don't know it any more. I have forgotten it. Leo was his surname. That was what everyone called him."

While I was still speaking, Lukas had seized a thick book from his writing-desk and was turning over the leaves. With amazing speed he found and put his finger on a place on an open page in the book. It was a directory, and where his finger lay stood the name Leo.

"Look," he laughed, "we already have a Leo. Andreas Leo, 69a Seilergraben. It is an unusual name; perhaps this man knows something about your Leo. Go and see him; perhaps he can tell you what you want to know. I can't say. Forgive me, my time is limited. I am very pleased to have seen you."

I reeled with stupefaction and excitement as I closed his door behind me. He was right. I could get nothing more from him.

On the very same day I went to Seilergraben, looked for the house and inquired about Mr. Andreas Leo. He lived in a room on the third floor. He was sometimes at home on Sundays and in the evenings; during the day he went to work. I inquired about his occupation. He did this, that and the other, they said; he could do manicures, chiropody and massage; he also made ointments and herbal cures. In bad times, when there was little to do, he sometimes also occupied himself by training and trimming dogs. I went away and decided it was better not to visit this man, or, at any rate, not to tell him of my intentions. Nevertheless, I was very curious to see him. I therefore watched the house during the next few days during my frequent walks, and I shall also go there today, for up till now I have not been successful in meeting Andreas Leo face to face.

Oh, the whole business is driving me to despair, and yet it makes me happy, or rather excited and eager. It gives importance to myself and my life again, and that had been very much lacking.

It is possible that the practitioners and psychologists who attribute all human action to egoistic desires are right; I cannot indeed see that a man who serves a cause all his life, who neglects his pleasures and well-being, and sacrifices himself for anything at all, really acts in the same way as a man who traffics in slaves or deals in munitions and squanders the proceeds on a life of pleasure. But no doubt I should immediately get the worst of it and be beaten in an argument with such a psychologist, for psychologists are, of course, people who always win. As far as I am concerned, they may be right. Then everything else that I have considered good and fine, and for which I have made sacrifices, has only been my egoistic desires. Indeed, every day I see my egoism more clearly in my plan to write some kind of history of the Journey to the East. At the beginning, it seemed to me that I was undertaking a laborious task in the name of a noble cause, but I see more and more that in the description of my journey I am only aiming at the same thing as Mr. Lukas with his war-book; namely, at saving my life by giving it meaning again.

If I could only see the way! If I could only make one step forward.

"Throw Leo overboard, free yourself from Leo!" Lukas said to me. I could just as much throw my head or my stomach overboard to get rid of them!

Dear God, help me a little.

IV

*

Now everything seems different again, and I do not yet know whether it has helped me in my problem or not. But I have had an experience, something has happened to me which I never expected—or no, did I not really expect it, did I not anticipate, hope for and really fear it? Yes, I did. Yet it remains strange and improbable enough.

I went to Seilergraben frequently, twenty times or more, at what I thought were favorable times, and often wandered past No. 69a, always with the thought, "I shall try once more, and if there is nothing in it I shall not come again." Yet I went again and again, and the day before yesterday my wish was fulfilled. Oh, and what a fulfillment it was.

As I approached the house of which I now knew every crack and fissure in its grey-green plaster, I heard the tune whistled of a little song or dance, a popular tune, coming from the upper window. I did not know anything yet, but I listened. The tune stirred my memory and some dormant recollections came to the fore. The music was banal but the whistling was wonderfully sweet, with soft and pleasing notes, unusually pure, as happy and as natural as the songs of birds. I stood and listened, enchanted, and at the same time strangely moved without, however, having any kind of accompanying thoughts. Or if I did, it was perhaps that it must be a very happy and amiable man who could whistle like that. For several minutes I stood there rooted to the spot and listened. An old man with a sick, sunken face went by. He saw me standing and listened too, just for a moment, then smiled at me with understanding as he went on. His beautiful, far-seeing old man's look seemed to say: "You stay there, one does not hear whistling like that every day." The old man's glance cheered me. I was sorry when he went past. At the same moment, however, I immediately realized that this whistling was the fulfillment of all my wishes, that the whistler must be Leo.

It was growing dark but there was still no light in any window. The tune, with its simple variations, was finished. There was silence. "He will now make a light up there," I thought, but everything remained in darkness. Then I heard a door being opened upstairs and soon I also heard footsteps on the stairs. The door of the house was opened and someone came out, and his walk was like his whistling, light and jolly, but steady, healthy and youthful. It was a very slim, hatless man, not very tall, who walked there, and now my feeling was changed to certainty. It was Leo; not only the Leo from the directory, it was Leo himself, our dear traveling companion and servant Leo, whose disappearance ten or

more years ago had brought us so much sadness and confusion. I nearly addressed him in
the moment of my initial joy and surprise.
Then I only just remembered that I had also
often heard him whistling during the journey
to the East. They were the same strains of
previous times, and yet how strangely different they sounded to me! A feeling of sadness
came over me like a stab in the heart: oh, how
different everything had become since then,
the sky, the air, the seasons, dreams, sleep, day
and night! How greatly and terribly everything had changed for me when, through
memory of the past alone, a whistle and the
rhythm of a known step could affect me so
deeply and give me so much pleasure and pain!

The man went close by me, his bare head,
supple and serene on his bare neck, appeared
above his blue open-neck shirt. The figure
moved easily and gaily along the darkening
lane, hardly audible in thin sandals or gym
shoes. I followed him without any particular
intention. How could I help but follow him!
He walked down the lane, and although his
step was light, effortless and youthful, it was

also in keeping with the evening; it was of the same quality as the twilight, it was friendly and at one with the hour, with the subdued sounds from the center of the town, with the half-light of the first lamps which were just beginning to appear.

He turned into the small park at St. Paul's Gate, disappeared amongst the tall round bushes, and I hurried so that I should not lose him. There he was again; he was sauntering slowly alongside the lilac bushes and the acacia. The path divided into two through the little wood. There were a couple of benches at the edge of the sward. Here under the trees it was already dark. Leo went past the first bench; a pair of lovers were sitting on it. The next bench was empty. He sat down, leaned against the bench, pressed his head back and for a time looked up at the foliage and the clouds. Then he took a small round white metal box out of his coat pocket, put it by his side on the bench, unscrewed the lid and slowly began to take something out of the box which he put into his mouth and ate with enjoyment. Meantime I walked to and from the entrance to the wood; I then went up to his bench and sat down at the other end. He looked up, gazed at me with clear grey eyes and went on eating. He was eating dried fruits, a few prunes and half apricots. He took them one after the other between two fingers, pressed and fingered each one a little, put them in his mouth and chewed them for a long time with enjoyment. It took a long time before he came to the last one and ate it. He then closed the box again and put it away, leaned back and stretched out his legs. I now saw that his cloth shoes had soles of plaited rope.

"It will rain tonight," he said suddenly, I knew not whether to me or to himself.

"Yes, it looks like it," I said, somewhat embarrassed, for as he had not yet recognized my figure and walk, it was possible and I was almost certain that he would now recognize me by my voice.

But no, he did not recognize me at all, not even by my voice, and although that had been my first wish, it nevertheless gave me a feeling of great disappointment. He did not recognize me. While he had remained the same after ten years and had apparently not aged at all, it was quite different with me, sadly different.

"You whistle very well," I said. "I heard you earlier on in Seilergraben. It gave me very much pleasure. I used to be a musician."

"Oh, were you!" he said in a friendly manner. "It's a great profession. Have you given it up?"

"Yes, for the time being. I have even sold my violin."

"Have you? What a pity! Are you in difficulties—that is to say, are you hungry? There is still some food at my house. I also have a little money in my purse."

"Oh, no," I said quickly, "I did not mean that. I am in quite good circumstances. I have more than I need. But thank you very much; it was very kind of you to make the offer. One does not often meet such kind people."

"Don't you think so? Well, maybe! People are often very strange. You are a strange person, too."

"Am I? Why?"

"Well, because you have enough money and yet you sell your violin. Don't you like music any more?"

"Oh, yes, but sometimes a man no longer finds pleasure in something he previously loved. Sometimes a man sells his violin or throws it against the wall, or a painter burns all his pictures. Have you never heard of such a thing?"

"Oh, yes. That comes from despair. It does happen. I even knew two people who committed suicide. Such people are stupid and can be dangerous. One just cannot help some people. But what do you do now that you no longer have your violin?"

"Oh, this, that and the other. I do not really do much. I am no longer young and I am also often ill. But why do you keep on talking about this violin? It is not really so important."

"The violin? It made me think of King David."

"King David? What has he to do with it?"

"He was also a musician. When he was quite young he used to play for King Saul and sometimes dispelled his bad moods with music. Later he became a king himself, a great king full of cares, having all sorts of moods and vexations. He wore a crown and conducted wars and all that kind of thing, and he also did many really wicked things and became very famous. But when I think of his life, the most beautiful part of it all is about the young David with his harp playing music to poor Saul, and it seems a pity to me that he later became a king. He was a much happier and better person when he was a musician."

"Of course he was!" I cried rather passionately. "Of course, he was younger then and more handsome and happier. But one does not always remain young; your David would in time have grown older and uglier and would have been full of cares even if he had remained a musician. So he became the great David, performed his deeds and composed his psalms. Life is not just a game!"

Leo then rose and bowed. "It is growing dark," he said, "and it will rain soon. I do not know a great deal more about the deeds that David performed, and whether they were really great. To be quite frank, I do not know very much more about his psalms either, but I should not like to say anything against them. But no account of David can prove to me that life is not just a game. That is just what life is when it is beautiful and happy—a game! Naturally, one can also do all kinds of other things with it, make a duty of it, or a battleground, or a prison, but that does not make it any prettier. Good-bye, pleased to have met you!"

This strange, lovable man began to move away in his light, steady and pleasing gait, and was on the point of disappearing when all my restraint and self-control broke down. I ran after him in despair and cried imploringly, "Leo! Leo! You are Leo, aren't you? Do you not know me any more? We were League brothers together and should still be so. We were both travelers on the journey to the East. Have you really forgotten me, Leo? Do you really no longer remember the Crown Watchers, Klingsor and Goldmund, the Festival in Bremgarten and the gorge at Morbio Inferiore? Leo, have pity on me!"

He did not run away as I had feared but he

also did not turn round; he walked steadily on as if he had heard nothing but gave me time to catch up to him, and did not seem to object to my joining him.

"You are so troubled and hasty," he said kindly, "that is not a good thing. It distorts the face and makes one ill. We shall walk quite slowly—it is so soothing. The few drops of rain are wonderful, aren't they? They come from the air like Eau de Cologne."

"Leo," I pleaded, "have pity! Tell me just one thing; do you know me yet?"

"Ah," he said kindly, and went on speaking as if to a sick or drunken man, "you will be better now; it was only excitement. You ask if I know you. Well, what person really knows another or even himself? As for me, I am not one who understands people at all. I am not interested in them. Now, I understand dogs quite well, and also birds and cats—but I don't really know you, sir."

"But do you not belong to the League? Did you not come on the journey with us?"

"I am still on the journey, sir, and I still belong to the League. So many come and go; one knows people and yet does not know them. It is much easier with dogs. Wait, stay here a moment!"

He raised a warning finger. We stood on the darkening garden-path which was becoming increasingly enveloped in a thin descending dampness. Leo pursed up his lips and sent out a long, vibrating, soft whistle, waited a while and whistled again. I drew back a little as, suddenly, close to us, behind the trellis-work railing at which we stood, a large Alsatian dog jumped out of the bushes and, whining with pleasure, pressed close to the fence in order to be stroked by Leo's fingers between the bars and wires. The powerful animal's eyes gleamed a light green, and whenever his glance alighted on me he growled deep down in his throat. It was like distant thunder, hardly audible.

"This is the Alsatian dog, Necker," said Leo, introducing me. "We are very good friends. Necker, here is a former violinist. You must not do anything to him, not even bark at him."

We stood there, and Leo gently scratched the dog's damp coat through the railing. It really was a pretty scene; it pleased me very much to see how friendly he was with the dog and the pleasure that this nocturnal greeting gave him. At the same time, it was painful to me and seemed hardly bearable that Leo should be so friendly with this Alsatian, and probably with many, perhaps with all the dogs in the district, while a world of aloofness separated him from me. The friendship and intimacy which I beseechingly and humbly sought seemed not only to belong to this dog Necker, but to every animal, to every raindrop, to every spot of ground on which Leo trod. He seemed to dedicate himself steadfastly and to rest continually in an easy, balanced relationship with his surroundings, knowing all things, known and beloved by all. Only with me, who loved and needed him so much, was there no contact, only from me did he dissociate himself; he regarded me in an unfriendly and cool fashion, was distant with me and had erased me from his memory.

We walked slowly on. On the other side of the railing the Alsatian accompanied him, making soft, contented sounds of affection and pleasure, but without forgetting my undesirable presence, for several times he suppressed his growling tone of defence and hostility for Leo's sake.

"Forgive me," I began again, "I am attaching myself to you and taking up your time. Naturally, you want to go home and go to bed."

"Not at all," he said with a smile. "I do not mind strolling along throughout the night like this. I am not lacking in either the time or the desire if it is not too much for you."

He said this in a very friendly manner and certainly without reservation. But he had hardly uttered the words when I suddenly felt in my head and in every muscle of my body how terribly tired I was, and how fatiguing every step of this futile and embarrassing nocturnal wandering was to me.

"I am really very tired," I said dejectedly, "I have only just realized it. There is also no sense in wandering about all night in the rain and being a nuisance to other people."

"As you wish," he said politely.

"Oh, Mr. Leo, you did not talk to me like

that during the League's journey to the East. Have you really forgotten all about it? Oh, well, it is no use. Do not let me keep you any longer. Good-night."

He disappeared quickly into the dark night. I remained alone, foolish, with my head bent. I had lost the game. He did not know me; he did not want to know me; he made fun of me.

I went back along the path; the dog Necker barked angrily behind the railing. I shivered from weariness, grief and loneliness in the damp warmth of the summer night.

I had experienced similar hours in the past. During such periods of despair it seemed to me as if I, a lost pilgrim, had reached the extreme edge of the world, and there was nothing left for me to do but to satisfy my last desire: to let myself fall from the edge of the world into the void—to death. In the course of time this despair returned many times; the compelling suicidal impulse, however, had been diverted and had almost vanished. Death was no longer nothingness, a void, negation. It had also become many other things to me. I now accepted the hours of despair as one accepts acute physical pain; one endures it, complainingly or defiantly; one feels it swell and increase, and sometimes there is a raging or mocking curiosity as to how much further it can go, to what extent the pain can still increase.

All the disgust for my disillusioned life which, since my return from the unsuccessful journey to the East, had become increasingly worthless and spiritless, all disbelief in myself and my abilities, all envious and regretful longing for the good and great times which I had once experienced, grew like a pain within me, grew as high as a tree, like a mountain, tugged at me, and was all related to the former task that I had begun, to the account of the Journey to the East and the League. It now seemed to me that even its accomplishment was no longer desirable or worthwhile. Only one hope still seemed worthwhile to me—to cleanse and redeem myself to some extent through my work, through my service to the memory of that great time, to bring myself once again into contact with the League and its experiences.

When I reached home I turned on the light, sat down at my desk in my wet clothes, my hat on my head, and wrote a letter. I wrote ten, twelve, twenty pages of grievances, remorse and entreaty to Leo. I described my need to him, conjured up images of our common experiences, of our former mutual friends. I bewailed the endless extreme difficulties which had shattered my noble enterprise. The weariness of the moment had disappeared; excited, I sat there and wrote. Despite all difficulties, I wrote, I would endure the worst possible thing rather than divulge a single secret of the League. Despite everything, I would not fail to complete my work in memory of the Journey to the East, in glorification of the League. As if in a fever, I covered page after page with hastily written words. The grievances, indictments and self-accusations tumbled from me like water from a breaking jug, without reflection, without faith, without hope of reply, only with the desire to unburden myself. While it was yet night I took the thick, confused letter to the nearest letter-box. Then, at last, it was nearly morning. I turned out the light, went to the small attic-bedroom next to my liv-ing-room and went to bed. I fell asleep immedi-ately and slept very deeply and for a long time.

V

*

After awakening and dozing off again several times, I awoke the following day with a headache but feeling rested. To my extreme astonishment, pleasure and also embarrassment, I found Leo in the living-room. He was sitting on the edge of a chair and looked as if he had been waiting a long time.

"Leo," I cried, "you have come!"

"They have sent me for you from the League," he said. "You wrote me a letter in connection with it. I gave it to the officials. You are to appear before the High Throne. Can we go?"

In confusion I hastened to put on my shoes. The desk, disarranged the previous night, still had a somewhat disturbed and disorderly appearance. For the moment I hardly knew any more what I had written there so forcibly and full of anguish a few hours ago. Still, it did not seem to have been in vain. Something had happened. Leo had come.

Suddenly, for the first time, I realized the significance of his words. So there was still a "League" of which I no longer knew anything, which existed without me and which no longer considered me as belonging to it! There was still a League and the High Throne! There were still the officials; they had sent for me! I went hot and cold at the realization. I had lived in this town many months, occupied with my notes about the League and our journey and did not know whether the rest of the League still existed, where it was, and whether I was perhaps its last member. Indeed, to be quite frank, at certain times I was not sure whether the League and my membership of it were ever real. And now Leo stood there, sent by the League to fetch me. I was remembered, I was summoned, they wanted to listen to me, perhaps to pass judgment on me. Good! I was ready. I was ready to show that I had not been unfaithful to the League. I was ready to obey. Whether the officials punished me or pardoned me, I was ready in advance to accept everything, to agree with their judgment in everything and to be obedient to them.

We set off. Leo went on ahead, and again, as I did many years ago when I watched him and the way he walked, I had to admire him as a good and perfect servant. He walked along the lanes in front of me, nimbly and patiently, indicating the way; he was the perfect guide, the perfect servant at his task, the perfect official. Yet he put my patience to no small test. The League had summoned me, I was awaited by the High Throne, everything was at stake for me; the whole of my future life would be decided, the whole of my past life would now either retain or completely lose its meaning— I trembled with expectation, pleasure, anxiety and suppressed fear. And so the route that Leo took seemed, in my impatience, intolerably long, for I had to follow my guide for more than two hours by way of the strangest and seemingly most capricious détours. Leo kept me waiting twice in front of a church in which he went to pray. For a long time that seemed endless to me, he remained meditating and absorbed in front of the old town-hall, and told me about its foundation in the fifteenth century by a famous member of the League. And although the way he took this walk seemed so painstaking, zealous and purposeful, I became quite confused by the détours, roundabouts and zig-zags by which he approached his goal. The walk, which took us all morning, could easily have been done in a quarter of an hour.

At last he led me into a sleepy, suburban lane, and into a very large, silent building. Outside it looked like an extended Council building or a museum. At first there was not a soul to be seen anywhere. Corridors and stairs were deserted and resounded at our footsteps. Leo began to search among the passages, stairs and antechambers. Once, he cautiously opened a big door, on the other side of which we saw a crowded artist's studio; in front of an easel stood the artist Klingsor in his shirt-sleeves— oh, how many years was it since I had seen his beloved face! But I did not dare to greet him; the time was not yet ripe for that. I was expected. I had been summoned. Klingsor did not pay very much attention to us. He nodded to Leo; either he did not see me or did not recognize me, and silently indicated to us in a friendly but decisive way to go out, not tolerating any interruption of his work.

Finally, at the top of the immense building, we arrived at a garret-storey, which smelled of paper and cardboard, and all along the walls for many hundreds of yards protruded cupboard-doors, backs of books and bundles of documents: a gigantic archive, a vast chancery. Nobody took any notice of us; everyone was silently occupied. It seemed to me as if the whole world, including the starry heavens, was governed or at least recorded and observed from there. For a long time we stood there and waited; many archive and library officials hastened around us silently with catalogue dockets and numbers in their hands. Ladders were placed in position and mounted, lifts and small trucks were carefully and quietly set into motion. Finally, Leo began to sing. I listened to the tune, deeply moved; it had once been very familiar to me. It was the melody of one of our League songs.

At the sound of the song, everything immediately sprang into movement. The officials drew back, the hall extended into dusky remoteness. The industrious people, small and unreal, worked in the gigantic archive region in the background. The foreground, however, was spacious and empty. The hall extended to an impressive length. In the middle, arranged in strict order, there were many benches, and partly from the background and partly out of the numerous doors came many officials who slowly approached the benches and one by one sat down on them. One row of benches after the other was slowly filled. The structure of benches gradually rose and culminated in a high throne, which was not yet occupied. The solemn Synedrium was crowded right up to the throne. Leo looked at me with a warning glance to be patient, silent and respectful, and disappeared amongst the crowd; all of a sudden he was gone and I could no longer see him. But here and there amidst the officials who assembled around the High Throne I perceived familiar faces, serious or smiling. I saw the figure of Albertus Magnus, the ferryman Vasudeva, the artist Klingsor, and others.

At last it became quiet and the Speaker stepped forward. Small and alone I stood before the High Throne, prepared for everything, in a state of great anxiety, but also in full accord with what would take place and be resolved here.

Clearly and evenly the Speaker's voice rang through the hall. "Self-accusation of a deserter League brother," I heard him announce. My knees trembled. It was a question of my life. But it was right that it should be so; everything must now be put in order. The Speaker continued.

"Is your name H.H.? Did you join in the march through Upper Swabia, and in the festival at Bremgarten? Did you desert your colors shortly after Morbio Inferiore? Did you confess that you wanted to write a story of the Journey to the East? Did you consider yourself hampered by your vow of silence about the League's secrets?"

I answered question after question with "Yes," even those which were incomprehensible and terrifying to me.

The officials conferred in whispers and with gestures for a short time; then the Speaker stepped forward again and announced:

"The self-accuser is herewith empowered to reveal publicly every law and secret of the League which is known to him. Moreover, the whole of the League's archives are placed at his disposal for his work."

The Speaker drew back. The officials disbanded and again slowly disappeared, some into the background of the hall and some through the exits; there was complete silence in the large hall. I was looking anxiously around me when I saw something lying on one of the chancery documents which seemed familiar to me. When I picked it up, I recognized my work, my delicate offspring, the manuscript I had commenced. "The Story of the Journey to the East," by H.H., was inscribed on the blue envelope. I seized it and read the small, close, hand-written, oft-times crossed out and corrected pages. In haste, eager to work, I was overwhelmed with the feeling that now at last, with approval from higher quarters, indeed assistance, I was to be allowed to complete my task. When I considered that no vow any longer bound me, that I had access to the archives, to those immense treasure-chambers, my task seemed to me greater and more worth-while than ever.

However, the more pages I read of my hand-writing, the less did I like the manuscript. Even in my former most despondent hours it had never seemed so futile and absurd to me as now. Everything seemed so confused and stupid; the clearest relationships were distorted, the most obvious were forgotten, the trivial and the unimportant pushed into the fore-ground. It must be written again, right from the beginning. As I continued reading the manuscript, I had to cross out sentence after sentence, and as I crossed them out, they crumbled up on the paper, and the clear, sloping letters separated into assorted fragments, into strokes and points, into circles, small flowers and stars, and the pages were covered like carpets with graceful, meaningless, ornamental designs. Soon there was nothing more left of my text; on the other hand, there was much unused paper left for my work. I pulled myself together. I tried to see things clearly. Naturally, it was not previously possible for me to present an impartial and clear account, because everything was concerned with secrets which I was forbidden to disclose on account of my vow to the League. I had tried to avoid an objective presentation of the story, and without regard to the more important relationships, aims and purposes, I had simply restricted myself to my personal experiences. But one could see where that had led. On the other hand, there was no longer a pledge of silence and no more restrictions. I was given complete official permission, and, moreover, the whole of the inexhaustible archives lay open to me.

It was clear to me that even if my former

work had not broken up into ornamentation, I had to begin the whole thing afresh, with a new foundation, and build it up again. I decided to begin with a short account of the League, its foundation and constitution. The extensive, endless, gigantic labelled catalogues on all the tables, which reached far into the distance and semi-darkness, must surely give an answer to all my questions.

First of all I decided to examine the archives at random. I had to learn how to use this tremendous machine. Naturally, I looked for the League document before anything else.

"League document," it stated in the catalogue, "see section Chrysostomos, group V, verse 39, 8."—Right, I found the section, the group and the verse quite easily. The archives were wonderfully arranged. And now I held the League document in my hand. I had to be prepared for the possibility that I might not be able to read it. As a matter of fact, I could not read it. It was written in Greek characters, it seemed to me, and I understood a certain amount of Greek, but for one thing it was in extremely ancient, strange writing, the characters of which, despite apparent clarity, were for the most part illegible to me, and, for another thing, the text was written in dialect or in a secret symbolical language, of which I only occasionally understood a word as if from a distance, by sound and analogy. But I was not yet discouraged. Even if the document remained unreadable, its characters brought back to me vivid memories of the past. In particular, I clearly saw my friend Longus writing Greek and Hebrew characters in the garden in the evening, the characters changing into birds, dragons and snakes in the night.

Looking through the catalogue, I trembled at the abundance of material that awaited me there. I came across many familiar words and many well-known names. With a start, I came across my own name, but I did not dare to consult the archives about it—who could bear to hear the verdict of an omniscient Court of Law on oneself? On the other hand, I found, for example, the name of the artist Paul Klee, whose acquaintance I had made during the journey and who was a friend of Klingsor's. I looked up his number in the archives. I found there a small gold-plated dish on which a clover was either painted or engraved. The first of its three leaves represented a small blue sailing-boat, the second a fish with colored scales and the third looked like a telegram-form on which was written:

As blue as snow,
*Is Paul like Klee.**

It also gave me a melancholy pleasure to read about Klingsor, Longus, Max and Tilli. Also I could not resist the desire to learn something more about Leo. On Leo's catalogue label was written:

Cave!
Archiepisc. XIX. Diacon. D. VII.
Corno Ammon. 6
Cave!

The two "Cave" warnings impressed me. I could not bring myself to penetrate this secret. However, with every new attempt, I began to

Note: *Klee=clover.

realize more and more what an undreamt-of abundance of material, knowledge and magic formulæ these archives contained. It included, it seemed to me, the whole world.

After happy or bewildering excursions into many branches of knowledge, I returned several times to the label "Leo" with ever-increasing curiosity. Each time the double "Cave" deterred me. Then, while going through another filing cabinet, I came across the word "Fatima," with the notes:

princ. orient. 2
noct. mill. 983
hort. delic. 07

I looked for and found the place in the archives. There lay a tiny locket which could be opened and contained a miniature portrait of a ravishingly beautiful princess, which in an instant reminded me of all the thousand and one nights, of all the tales of my youth, of all the dreams and wishes of that great period when, in order to travel to Fatima in the Orient, I had

served my novitiate and had reported myself
as a member of the League. The locket was
wrapped in a finely-spun mauve silk kerchief,
which had an immeasurably remote and sweet
fragrance, reminiscent of princesses and the
East. As I inhaled this remote, rare, magic
fragrance, I was suddenly and powerfully overwhelmed with the realization of the sweet
magic which had enveloped me when I commenced my pilgrimage to the East, and how
the pilgrimage was shattered by treacherous
and, in fact, unknown obstacles, how the
magic had then vanished more and more, and
what desolation, disillusionment and barren
despair had since been my life's breath, my
food and drink! I could no longer see the kerchief or the portrait, so thick was the veil of
tears which covered my eyes. Ah, now, I
thought, the portrait of the Arabian princess
could no longer suffice to act as a charm against
the world and hell, and make me into a knight
and crusader; I would now need other stronger
charms. But how sweet, how innocent, how
blissful had been that dream which had

haunted my youth, which had made me a story-teller, a musician and a novitiate, and had led me to Morbio!

Sounds awakened me from my meditation. From all sides the unending spaciousness of the archive chamber confronted me eerily. A new thought, a new pain shot threw me like a flash of lightning. I, in my simplicity, wanted to write the story of the League, I, who could not decipher or understand one-thousandth part of those millions of scripts, books, pictures and references in the archives! Humbled, unspeakably foolish, unspeakably ridiculous, not understanding myself, feeling extremely small, I saw myself standing in the midst of this thing with which I had been allowed to play a little in order to make me realize what the League was and what I was myself.

The officials came through the numerous doors in enormous numbers. I could still recognize many of them through my tears. I recognized Jup, the magician, I recognized Lindhorst, the archivist, I recognized Mozart dressed as Pablo. The illustrious assembly filled the many rows of seats, which became higher and narrower at the back; over the throne which formed the top, I saw a shining golden canopy.

The Speaker stepped forward and announced: "The League is ready to pass judgment, through its officials, on the self-accuser H., who felt bound to keep silent about League secrets, and who has now realized how strange and blasphemous was his intention to write the story of a journey to which he was not equal, and an account of a League in whose existence he no longer believed and to which he had become unfaithful."

He turned towards me and said in his clear, proclamatory voice: "Self-accuser H., do you agree to recognize the Court of Justice and to submit to its judgment?"

"Yes," I replied.

"Self-accuser H.," he continued, "do you agree that the Court of Justice of the officials pass judgment on you without the President in the Chair, or do you desire the President himself to pass judgment on you."

"I agree," I said, "to be judged by the officials, either with or without the President in the Chair."

The Speaker was about to reply when, from the very back of the hall, a soft voice said: "The President is ready to pass judgment himself."

The sound of this soft voice shook me strangely. Right from the depths of the room, from the remote horizons of the archives, came a man. His walk was light and peaceful, his robe sparkled with gold. He came nearer amid the silence of the assembly, and I recognized his walk, I recognized his movements, and finally I recognized his face. It was Leo. In a magnificent, festive robe, he climbed through the rows of officials to the High Throne like a Pope. Like a magnificent, rare flower, he carried the brilliance of his attire up the stairs. Each row of officials rose to greet him as he passed. He bore his radiant office conscientiously, humbly, dutifully, as humbly as a holy Pope or patriarch bears his insignia.

I was deeply intrigued and moved in anticipation of the judgment which I was humbly prepared to accept, whether it would now bring punishment or grace. I was no less deeply moved and amazed that it was Leo, the former porter and servant, who now stood at the head of the whole League and was ready to pass judgment on me. But I was still more stirred, amazed, startled and happy at the great discovery of the day: that the League was as completely stable and mighty as ever, that it was not Leo and the League who had deserted and disillusioned me, but only that I had been so weak and foolish as to misinterpret my own experiences, to doubt the League, to consider the Journey to the East a failure, and to regard myself as the survivor and chronicler of a concluded and forgotten tale, while I was nothing more than a run-away, a traitor, a deserter. Amazement and joy lay in this recognition. I stood there, small and humble, at the foot of the High Throne, from which I had once been accepted as a brother of the League, from which I had once undergone my novitiate ceremony, had received the League ring and had immediately been sent to the servant Leo on the journey. And in the middle of everything, I was aware of a new sin, a new inexplicable loss, a new shame: I no longer possessed the League ring. I had lost it, I did not know when or where, and I had not missed it once until this day!

Meantime, the President, the golden-clad Leo, began to speak in his beautiful, gentle voice; his words reached me gently and comfortingly, as gentle and comforting as sunshine.

"The self-accuser," came the words from the High Throne, "has had the opportunity to rid himself of some of his errors. There is much to be said against him. It may be conceivable and very excusable that he was unfaithful to the League, that he reproached the League with his own failings and follies, that he doubted its continuation, that he had the strange ambition to become the historian of the League. All this does not weigh heavily against him. They are, if the self-accuser will permit me the phrase, only novitiate stupidities. They can be dismissed with a smile."

I breathed deeply and a faint smile passed over the whole of the illustrious assembly. That the most serious of my sins, even my illusion that the League no longer existed and that

I was the only disciple left, were only regarded by the President as "stupidities," as trifles, was a tremendous relief to me and at the same time sent me most definitely back to my starting-point.

"But," continued Leo, and his gentle voice was now sad and serious—"there are many more serious offences imputed to the defendant and the worst of them is that he does not stand as self-accuser for these sins, but appears to be unaware of them. He deeply regrets having wronged the League in thought; he cannot forgive himself for not recognizing the President Leo in the servant Leo, and is on the point of realizing the extent of his infidelity to the League. But while he took these sinful thoughts and follies all too seriously, and only just realizes with relief that they can be dismissed with a smile, he stubbornly forgets his real offences, which are legion, each one of which is serious enough to warrant severe punishment."

My heart beat quickly. Leo turned towards me. "Defendant H., later you will have insight to your errors and you will also be shown how to avoid them in future. But just to show you what little understanding you still have of your position, I ask you: Do you remember your walk through the town accompanied by the servant Leo, who, as messenger, had to bring you before the High Throne? Yes, you remember. And do you remember how we passed the Town Hall, the Church of St. Paul and the Cathedral, and how the servant Leo entered the Cathedral in order to kneel and pray awhile, and how you not only refrained from entering with me to perform your devotions in accordance with the fourth precept of your League vow, but how you remained outside, impatient and bored, waiting for the end of the tedious ceremony which seemed so unnecessary to you, which was nothing more to you than a disagreeable test of your egoistic impatience? Yes, you remember. By your behavior at the Cathedral gate alone, you have already trampled on the fundamental requirements and customs of the League. You have slighted religion, you have been contemptuous towards a League brother, you have impatiently rejected an opportunity and invitation to prayer and meditation. These sins would be unforgivable were there not special extenuating circumstances in your case."

He had now struck home. Everything would now be said; there would be no more secondary issues, no more mere stupidities. He was more than right. He had struck at my heart.

"We do not want to count up all the defendant's errors," continued the President, "he is not going to be judged according to the letter, and we know that it only needed our reminder to awaken the defendant's conscience and make him a repentant self-accuser."

"Just the same, self-accuser H., I would advise you to bring some of your other acts before the judgment of your conscience. Must I remind you of the evening when you visited the servant Leo and wished to be recognized by him as a League brother, although this was impossible, for you had made yourself unrecognizable as a League brother? Must I remind you of things which you yourself said to the servant Leo? About the sale of your violin? About the dreadful, stupid, narrow, suicidal life which you have led for years?

"There is still one more thing, League brother H., about which I should not keep silent. It is quite possible that the servant Leo did you an injustice that evening. Let us suppose that he did. The servant Leo was perhaps too strict, perhaps too rational; perhaps he did not show enough forbearance and sympathy towards you and your circumstances. But there are higher authorities and more infallible judges than the servant Leo. What was the animal's judgment on you, defendant? Do you remember the dog Necker? Do you remember his rejection and condemnation of you? He is incorruptible, he does not takes sides, he is not a League brother."

He paused. Yes, the Alsatian Necker! He had certainly rejected me and condemned me. I agreed. Judgment was already passed on me by the Alsatian, already by myself.

"Self-accuser H.," began Leo again, and from the golden gleam of his robes and canopy his voice now rang out cool and bright and clear, like the voice of the commandant when he appears before Don Giovanni's door in the last Act. "Self-accuser H., you have listened to me. You have agreed with me. You have, we presume, already passed judgment on yourself?"

"Yes," I said in a soft voice, "yes."

"It is, we presume, an unfavorable judgment which you have passed on yourself?"

"Yes," I whispered.

Leo then rose from the throne and gently stretched out his arms.

"I now turn to you, my officials. You have heard and know how things have been with League brother H. It is a lot that is not unfamiliar to you; many of you have had to experience it yourselves. The defendant did not know until this hour, or could not really believe, that his apostasy and aberration were a test. For a long time he did not give in. He endured it for many years, knowing nothing about the League, remaining alone, and seeing everything in which he believed in ruins. Finally, he could no longer hide and contain himself. His suffering became too great, and you know that as soon as suffering becomes acute enough, one goes forward. Brother H. was led to despair in his test, and despair is the result of each earnest attempt to understand and vindicate human life. Despair is the result of each earnest attempt to go through life with virtue, justice and understanding and to fulfil their requirements. Children live on one side of despair, the awakened on the other side. Defendant H. is no longer a child and is not yet fully awakened. He is still in the midst of despair. He will overcome it and thereby go through his second novitiate. We welcome him anew into the League, the meaning of which he no longer claims to understand. We give back to him his lost ring, which the servant Leo has kept for him."

The Speaker then brought the ring, kissed me on the cheek and placed the ring on my finger. Hardly had I looked at the ring, hardly had I felt its metallic coolness on my fingers, when a thousand things occurred to me, a thousand inconceivable acts of neglect. Above all, it occurred to me that the ring had four stones at equal distances apart, and that it was a rule of the League and part of the vow to turn the ring slowly on the finger at least once a day, and at each of the four stones to bring to mind one of the four basic precepts of the vow. I had not only lost the ring and had not once missed it, but during all those dreadful years I had also no longer repeated the four basic precepts or thought of them. Immediately, I tried to say them again inwardly. I had an idea what they were, they were still within me, they belonged to me as does a name which one will remember in a moment but at that particular moment cannot be recalled. No, it remained silent within me, I could not repeat the rules, I had forgotten the wording. I had forgotten the rules; for many years I had not repeated them, for many years I had not observed them and held them sacred—and yet I had considered myself a loyal League brother.

The Speaker patted my arm kindly when he observed my dismay and deep shame. Then I heard the President speak again:

"Defendant and self-accuser H., you are acquitted, but I have to tell you that it is the duty of a brother who is acquitted in such a case to enter the ranks of the officials and occupy one of their seats as soon as he has passed a test of his faith and obedience. He has the option of choosing the test. Now, brother H., answer my questions!

"Are you prepared to tame a wild dog as a test of your faith?"

I drew back in horror.

"No, I could not do it," I cried, moving away.

"Are you prepared and willing to burn the League's archives immediately at our command, as our Speaker burns a portion of them now before your eyes?"

The Speaker stepped forward, plunged his hands into the well-arranged filing-cabinets, drew out both hands full of papers, many hundreds of papers, and to my horror burnt them over a coal-pan.

"No," I said, drawing back, "I could not do that either."

"Cave, frater," cried the President. "Take heed, impetuous brother! I have begun with the easiest tasks which require the smallest amount of faith. Each succeeding task will be increasingly difficult. Answer me: are you prepared and willing to consult our archives about yourself?"

I went cold and held my breath, but I had understood. Each question would become more and more difficult; there was no escape except into what was still worse. Breathing deeply, I stood up and said yes.

The Speaker led me to the tables where the hundreds of filing-cabinets stood. I looked for and found the letter H. I found my name and, indeed, first of all that of my ancestor Eoban, who, four hundred years ago, had also been a member of the League. Then there was my own name, with the comment:

Chattorum r. gest. XC.
civ. Calv. infid. 49.

The sheet shook in my hand. Meanwhile, the officials rose from their seats one after the other, held out their hands to me, looked me straight in the face, then went away. The High Throne was vacated and, last of all, the President descended the throne, held out his hand to me, looked me in the face, smiled his pious, kind bishop's smile and left the hall last of all. I remained there alone, the note in my hand to refer to the archives for information.

I could not immediately bring myself to take the step of consulting the archives about myself. I stood hesitating in the empty hall and saw extending for a long way the boxes, cupboards, pigeon-holes and cabinets, the accumulation of all the worth-while knowledge to which I could ever gain access. Yet as much from fear of seeing my own record sheet as from a burning desire for knowledge, I allowed my own affairs to wait a little in order to learn first about one thing and another which was important to me and my story of the journey to the East. To be sure, I had long really known that my story had already been condemned and disposed of and that I should never finish writing it. Just the same, I was curious.

I noticed a badly-filed memorandum projecting from amongst the others in one of the filing-cabinets. I went towards it and drew out the memorandum on which was written:

Morbio Inferiore.

No other catch-word could have expressed
the extent of my curiosity more briefly and accurately. With my heart beating quickly, I
looked up the place in the archives. It was a
section of the archives which contained a
rather large number of papers. On the top lay
a copy of a description of the Morbio Gorge
taken from an old Italian book, then there
was a quarto sheet with short notes on the
part which Morbio had played in the history
of the League. All the notes referred to the
Journey to the East and indeed to the base
and group to which I had belonged. Our
group, it was recorded here, had arrived at
Morbio on its journey. There it was submitted
to a test which it did not pass, namely, the
disappearance of Leo. Although the League's
rules should have guided us, and although
even in the event of a League group remaining
without a leader, the precepts held good and
had been inculcated in us at the beginning of
the journey, yet from the moment our whole
group discovered the disappearance of Leo it

had lost its head and faith, had entertained doubts and entered into futile arguments. In the end, the whole group, contrary to the spirit of the League, had broken up into factions and disbanded. This explanation of the disaster of Morbio could no longer surprise me much. On the other hand, I was extremely surprised at what I read further on about the breaking-up of our group, namely, that no less than three of our League brothers had made an attempt to write an account of our journey and had given a description of the events at Morbio. I was one of these three and a fair copy of my manuscript was included in the section. I read through the two others with the strangest feelings. Basically, both writers described the events of that day not very differently from the way I had done, and yet how different they seemed to me! I read in one of them:

"It was the absence of the servant Leo which revealed to us, suddenly and terribly, the extent of the dissention and the perplexities which shattered our hitherto apparent complete unity. A few of us, to be sure, immediately knew or suspected that Leo had neither come to any harm nor run away, but that he had secretly been recalled by the League officials. Yet not one of us can contemplate without feelings of deepest repentance and shame how badly we underwent this test. Hardly had Leo left us, when faith and concord amongst us was at an end; it was as if the life-blood of our group flowed away from an invisible wound. First there were differences of opinion, then open quarrels about the most futile and ridiculous questions. For example, I remember that our very popular and praiseworthy choirmaster H.H. suddenly maintained that the missing Leo had also taken in his bag, along with other valuable objects, the ancient sacred document, the original manuscript of the Master. This statement was heatedly disputed for days. Treated symbolically, H.'s absurd assertion was really remarkably significant; indeed, it did seem as if the prosperity of the League, the cohesion of the whole, was completely gone with Leo's departure from our little group. The very same musician H. was a sad example of this. Until the day of Morbio Inferiore he was one of the most loyal and faithful League brothers, as well as popular as an artist, and, despite many weaknesses of character, he was one of our most active members. But he relapsed into brooding, depression and mistrust, became more than negligent in his duties, and began to be intolerant, nervous and quarrelsome. As he finally remained behind on the march one day and did not appear again, it did not occur to anyone to stop on his behalf and look for him; it was evidently a case of desertion. Unfortunately, he was not the only one, and finally nothing was left of our little traveling group. . . ."

I found this passage in the other historian's work:

"Just as ancient Rome collapsed after Cæsar's death, or democratic thought throughout the world on Wilson's desertion of the colors, so did our League break up on the unhappy day of Morbio. As far as blame and responsibility can be mentioned, two apparently harmless members were to blame for the collapse, the musician H.H. and Leo, one of the servants. These two men were previously popular and faithful members of the League, although lacking in understanding of its significance in world history. They disappeared one day without leaving any trace, taking with them many valuable possessions and important documents, which indicates that both wretches were bribed by enemies of the League. . . ."

If the memory of this historian was so very confused and inaccurate, although he apparently made the report in all good faith and with the conviction of its complete veracity—what was the value of my own notes? If ten other accounts by other authors were found about Morbio, Leo and myself, they would presumably all contradict and censure each other. No, our historical efforts were of no use; there was no point in continuing with them and reading them; one could quietly let them be covered with dust in this section of the archives.

A shudder went through me at the thought of what I should still learn in this hour. How awry, altered and distorted everything and everyone was in these mirrors, how mockingly and unattainably did the face of truth hide itself behind all these reports, counter-reports and legends! What was still truth? What was still credible? And what would remain when I also learned about myself, about my own character and history from the knowledge stored in these archives?

I must be prepared for anything. Suddenly I could bear the uncertainty and suspense no longer. I hastened to the section Chattorum res gestæ, looked for my sub-division and number and stood in front of the part marked with my name. This was a niche, and when I drew the thin curtains aside I saw that it contained nothing written. It contained nothing but a figure, an old and worn-looking model made from wood or wax, in pale colors. It appeared to be a kind of deity or barbaric idol. At first glance it was entirely incomprehensible to me. It was a figure that really consisted of two; it had a common back. I stared at it for a while, disappointed and surprised. Then I noticed a candle in a metal candlestick fixed to the wall of the niche. A match-box lay there. I lit the candle and the strange double figure was now brightly illuminated.

Only slowly did it dawn upon me. Only

slowly and gradually did I begin to suspect and then perceive what it was intended to represent. It represented a figure which was myself, and this likeness of myself was unpleasantly weak and half-real; it had blurred features, and in its whole expression there was something unstable, weak, dying or wishing to die, and looked rather like a piece of sculpture which could be called "Transitoriness" or "Decay," or something similar. On the other hand, the other figure which was joined to mine to make one, was strong in color and form, and just as I began to realize whom it resembled, namely, the servant and President Leo, I discovered a second candle in the wall and lit this also. I now saw the double figure representing Leo and myself, not only becoming clearer and each image more alike, but I also saw that the surface of the figures was transparent and that one could look inside as one can look through the glass of a bottle or vase. Inside the figures I saw something moving, slowly, extremely slowly, in the same way that a snake moves which has fallen asleep. Something was taken place there, something

117

like a very slow, smooth but continuous flowing or melting; indeed, something melted or poured across from my image to that of Leo's. I perceived that my image was in the process of adding to and flowing into Leo's, nourishing and strengthening it. It seemed that, in time, all the substance from one image would flow into the other and only one would remain: Leo. He must grow, I must disappear.

As I stood there and looked and tried to understand what I saw, I recalled a short conversation that I had once had with Leo during the festive days at Bremgarten. We had talked about the creations of poetry being more vivid and real than the poets themselves.

The candles burned low and went out. I was overcome by an infinite weariness and desire to sleep, and I turned away to find a place where I could lie down and sleep.